This book belongs to:

....

....

For Alex

A TEMPLAR BOOK
First published in the UK in 2021 by Templar Books,
an imprint of Bonnier Books UK,
The Plaza, 535 King's Road, London, SW10 0SZ
Owned by Bonnier Books, Sveavägen 56, Stockholm, Sweden
www.templarco.co.uk · www.bonnierbooks.co.uk

Text and illustration copyright © 2021 by Frann Preston Gannon
Design copyright © 2021 by Templar Books

2 4 6 8 10 9 7 5 3 1

All rights reserved

ISBN 978-1-78741-684-0

Edited by Katie Haworth
Designed by Genevieve Webster
Production by Ella Holden
Printed in China

FSC
www.fsc.org

MIX
Paper from
responsible sources
FSC® C104723

Bird's Eye View

Frann Preston-Gannon

templar
books

Little Bird lived in a nest with her mama
at the top of a tall tree.

It was safe and warm, but she was curious about
life beyond the forest.

"What is beyond the treetops?"
she asked her mama.

"Well, child . . ." Mama said. "People live there.
My own mother told me to stay away from them and so I did."
"But what *are* people?" asked Little Bird.
Mama didn't know.

Little Bird's curiosity kept growing and as soon
as her wings were strong enough she said,
"Mama, I am off to see the world."

"Goodbye, my love," said Mama. "Please be careful!"

Little Bird soared and swooped over the treetops.
She had never felt such freedom!

Before long, she saw something floating on a lake.

"Ahh, this must be people!" Little Bird said.
"They seem quiet and slow."

Soon, she came to a place where boxes were scattered over the land.
There were people all around.

Those boxes must be their nests,
she thought.

The nests grew higher and higher,
and now the people seemed to be in such a hurry! Perhaps they
were not that quiet and slow after all?

Little Bird saw many people.

They were colourful and happy . . .   they were sharing . . .

and they sang beautiful songs,
just like birds!

Then Little Bird saw
something that worried her.

There were other birds,
but they could not fly.

"Why are you locked up?"
Little Bird asked.

"People put us here,"
they said. "Fly away,
Little Bird! It is
not safe!"

So she did.

She flew as fast as she could.

When she looked down, she saw
that everything was dirty.

There were mountains of rubbish and a smoke-stained sky.
"Yuck," said Little Bird. "How messy people are!"

But soon she saw other people . . .
and these ones were cleaning the mess up!
"People are confusing!" said Little Bird.

She kept flying. Soon, she was over the ink-blue ocean.
It seemed to go on forever! She began to wish she was back home.

At last she reached a new shore and
found the nests of other people.
These ones were broken.

The people were on the move.
"They are migrating like birds!" she said.
"They look as tired as I feel."

She flew away from that place and saw people wherever she went.

Some were changing the land below her . . .

and others were fast and busy.

They could be loud
and together . . .

or quiet
and lonely.

Many seemed playful
and friendly.

Finally, she had to rest. Her head was spinning! She had seen so many people
and they were so many different things. Then, suddenly . . .

Little Bird saw a net!

Memories of cages filled
her mind and she flew away
with all her strength,
up and up . . .

. . . then down
and down.

Little Bird was hurt.
She wondered if she would ever
see her mama again.

But then, little hands gently picked her up.

The little hands belonged to little people
who took the bird somewhere safe to rest.

Soon, her wing felt
much better and the kind
people helped her on her way.

She sang goodbye with
the sweetest song she knew.

Little Bird had seen so much of the world
and now she longed to be back safe and warm in her nest.

She hoped she would remember the way home.

But soon, a familiar forest became a familiar tree . . .

and that became a familiar branch.

"Hello, my love," said Mama. "I have missed you."
"I missed you too, Mama! I met people!" said Little Bird.
"What were they like?" asked Mama with wonder.

"They were many, many things,"
said Little Bird.
"But the ones I will remember most
are the ones that were kind."

Also available:

ISBN: 978-1-78741-660-4

ISBN: 978-1-78741-386-3